Text: Udo Weigelt
Illustrations: Nina Spranger
Copyright © 2006 Patmos Verlag GmbH & Co. KG, Sauerländer Verlag, Düsseldorf
Translation copyright © 2007 by Patmos Verlag GmbH & Co. KG
First published as *Wundermeerschwein rettet die Welt* in 2006 by Patmos Verlag GmbH & Co. KG

Published in the United States of America in 2007 by Walker Publishing Company, Inc.
Distributed to the trade by Holtzbrinck Publishers

For information about permission to reproduce selections from this book,
write to Permissions, Walker & Company, 104 Fifth Avenue, New York, New York 10011

Library of Congress Cataloging-in-Publication Data
available upon request
ISBN-13: 978-0-8027-9705-6 • ISBN-10: 0-8027-9705-9 (hardcover)
ISBN-13: 978-0-8027-9706-3 • ISBN-10: 0-8027-9706-7 (reinforced)

The art for this book was created with watercolor and acrylic paints on watercolor paper.
Typeset in Humana Sans.

Visit Walker & Company's Web site at www.walkeryoungreaders.com

Printed in China
10 9 8 7 6 5 4 3 2 1 (hardcover)
10 9 8 7 6 5 4 3 2 1 (reinforced)

All papers used by Walker & Company are natural, recyclable products made
from wood grown in well-managed forests. The manufacturing processes
conform to the environmental regulations of the country of origin.

SUPER GUINEA PIG TO THE RESCUE

Udo Weigelt
Illustrations by Nina Spranger

Walker & Co.
New York

The Cohen family had four pets: a yellow canary, an old hound dog, a plump goldfish, and a little guinea pig.

They were all very good friends and liked to watch television together. The TV in the living room was always on, even if there was no one watching it.

The one who liked to watch it most of all was the little guinea pig. His favorite show was *Super Guinea Pig to the Rescue*. Every day Super Guinea Pig saved the world from evil and terrible disasters! And every day the little guinea pig tuned in to watch his hero.

"A guinea pig that saves the world? Ridiculous!" said the old hound dog.

"He can't really fly! How silly," said the yellow canary.

The plump goldfish gurgled in agreement.

"You're just jealous," yelled the little guinea pig, "because only other guinea pigs can call him for help just by thinking about him. And just so you know, he's my best friend!"

"Ah, your *best* friend. Right," said the canary.

"Go ahead and call your best friend. We'd like to see him," said the hound dog.

"Blub," added the goldfish.

"Okay, you asked for it," said the little guinea pig. "But I'm warning you, he's not going to like what you've been saying about him."

And with that, the little guinea pig ran out of the living room.

With all his might, the little guinea pig thought about Super Guinea Pig and wished he would show up.

"I need you here to show my other friends that you do exist," thought the little guinea pig.

But Super Guinea Pig did not come.

Spying a napkin on the counter, the little guinea pig got an idea. He put on the red napkin like a cape. He nibbled at a black sock to create a superhero mask and belt. And he attached a pin to his belt like a sword.

The little guinea pig practiced his moves. He jumped, he swung
his sword, and he admired his new look in the mirror.

He was . . .
Super Guinea Pig!

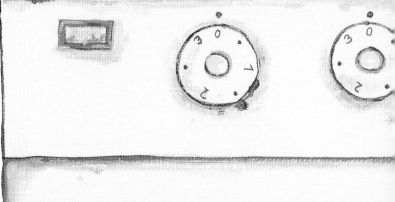

The little guinea pig jumped through the living room doorway and startled his friends. "Who dares to doubt Super Guinea Pig?"

"I don't believe it! Super Guinea Pig has jumped out of the television," shouted the old hound dog.

"No way," screeched the canary.

"Blub, blub," said the goldfish.

"So you thought you could make fun of me?" asked Super Guinea Pig
as he waved his sword. "I will fix all of you evil creatures."

The old hound dog just rolled his eyes.

The yellow canary ignored him and flew away over his head.

And the plump goldfish made a bubbling noise.

"Ha! You can't run from me! I'll find you wherever you hide," shouted Super Guinea Pig. He chased after the canary. But when he tried to jump up on a high shelf, he suddenly lost his balance! He fell

down,

down,

down . . .

. . . and landed with a giant splash right in the goldfish bowl.

"Help!" he shouted. "I can't swim!" In his mind, the little guinea pig called for the real Super Guinea Pig again. "Please, I really need your help right now! Save me!"

But Super Guinea Pig did not come.

The canary shouted to the old hound dog, "The little guinea pig has fallen into the goldfish bowl. He needs your help!"

So the old hound dog rescued him from the water.

The little guinea pig said nothing and quickly ran to his cage, soggy and embarrassed.

The little guinea pig dried himself off and thought about what had happened. Finally, he took a deep breath and went into the living room.

"Hi, guys! Want to play a game?" he asked carefully.

"Now? Your best friend, Super Guinea Pig, is on television soon," said the old hound dog.

"Oh, him?" said the little guinea pig. "He's just on television. He's not a *real* friend."

The old hound dog and the yellow canary winked at each other. And the goldfish blubbed.